For anyone who isn't sure if they matter.
You do.

ATHENEUM BOOKS FOR YOUNG READERS • An imprint of Simon & Schuster Children's Publishing Division • 1230 Avenue of the Americas, New York, New York 10020 • Copyright © 2020 by Christian Robinson • All rights reserved, including the right of reproduction in whole or in part in any form. • ATHENEUM BOOKS FOR YOUNG READERS is a registered trademark of Simon & Schuster, Inc. Atheneum logo is a trademark of Simon & Schuster, Inc. • For information about special discounts for bulk purchases, please contact Simon & Schuster Special Sales at 1-866-506-1949 or business@simonandschuster.com. • The Simon & Schuster Speakers Bureau can bring authors to your live event. For more information or to book an event, contact the Simon & Schuster Speakers Bureau at 1-866-248-3049 or visit our website at www.simonspeakers.com. • Book design by Sonia Chaghatzbanian • The text for this book was hand-lettered. • The illustrations for this book were rendered in acrylic paint and collage. • Manufactured in China • 1120 SCP • 10 9 8 7 6 5 4 • Library of Congress Cataloging-in-Publication • Names: Robinson, Christian, author, illustrator. • Title: You matter / Christian Robinson. • Description: First edition. | New York : Atheneum Books for Young Readers, [2020] | Audience: Ages 4–8. | Audience: Grades K–1. | Summary: Illustrations and easy-to-read text remind the reader that no matter what happens or how one feels, he or she matters. • Identifiers: LCCN 2019043812 (print) | LCCN 2019043813 (eBook) | ISBN 9781534421691 (hardcover) | ISBN 9781534421707 (eBook) • Subjects: CYAC: Self-esteem—Fiction. | Self-acceptance—Fiction. • Classification: LCC PZ7.1.R6363 You 2020 (print) | LCC PZ7.1.R6363 (eBook) | DDC [E]—dc23 • LC record available at https://lccn.loc.gov/2019043812 • LC eBook record available at https://lccn.loc.gov/2019043813

you matter

christian robinson

A atheneum books for young readers
atheneum new york london toronto sydney new delhi

The small stuff too small to see.

Those who swim with the tide

and those who don't.

The first to go and the last.

You matter.

When everyone thinks you're a pest.

When something is just out of reach.

When everyone is too busy to help.

You matter.

If you fall down.

If you have to start all over again.

Even if you are really gassy.

You matter.

Sometimes home is far away.

Sometimes someone you love says good-bye.

Sometimes you feel lost and alone.

But you matter.

Old and young.

The first to go and the last.

The small stuff too small to see.

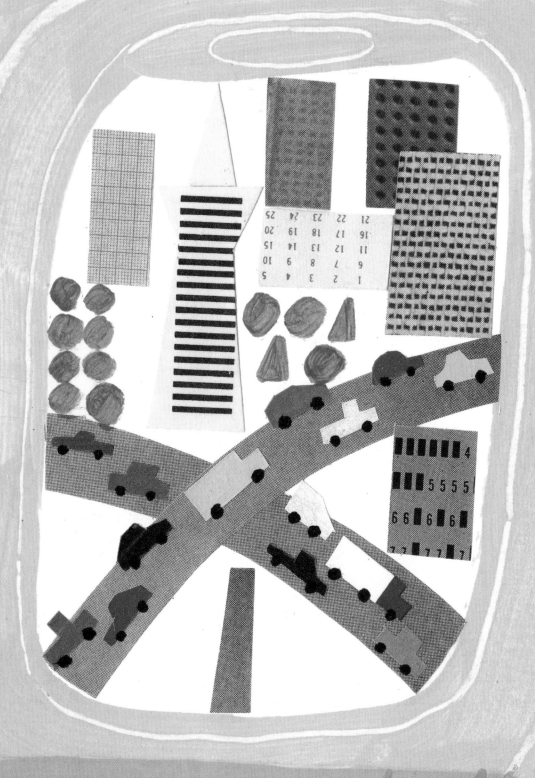

You matter.